First published in Great Britain 1984 by
Hamish Hamilton Children's Books
Garden House, 57–59 Long Acre, London WC2E 9JZ
Copyright © 1984 by Nigel Snell
All Rights Reserved

British Library Cataloguing in Publication Data

Snell, Nigel
Jason breaks his arm
1. Children – Hospital care – Juvenile
literature
I. Title
362.1'9892   RJ27
ISBN 0-241-11296-6

Printed in Great Britain by
Cambus Litho, East Kilbride

Jason Breaks His Arm

NIGEL SNELL

Hamish Hamilton · London

Jason had lots of friends.
They lived near a big park with
trees and a large lake.

Jason and his friends loved
climbing trees.
Their favourite tree had a rope
hanging down from it.
It was great fun swinging
over the little ditch below.

One day, four boys held
on to the rope together.
They started to scream as
they swung out over the ditch.
One by one they fell off.
Jason was the last to fall.

He fell heavily into the ditch and landed on his arm.

His arm was very painful.
He felt sick and dizzy, and
it was difficult to move his fingers.

One of his friends ran off
to get Jason's Mummy.
She called an ambulance, and soon
Jason was on his way to hospital.

At the hospital, a special kind of
photograph (called an X-ray)
was taken of his arm.

Later on, a doctor looked at the X-ray.
She said Jason had broken his arm.

'We'll have to put you in plaster,
young man,' she said.
'Then your arm will heal more quickly.'

'We've got plasters at home,' said Jason.
The doctor told him this one was different.

Jason was wheeled along a long passage, and into a small room.

'We're going to make you go to sleep,' said the doctor.

'Then you won't feel anything when we put on the plaster.'

Another doctor pricked his hand with a little needle.

The next thing Jason knew, he was in bed.
There were lots of other children
in the ward. Most of them were in bed, too.

Jason had a large white plaster
on his arm.
It felt hard and stiff.
He was very proud of it.
He showed it to his Mummy and Daddy.

Jason spent the night in hospital.
When he came home the next day,
all his friends came round to see him.
They wrote their names on his plaster.

A few days later, Jason went back
to the hospital for another X-ray.
The doctor told him she would take off
the plaster in a few weeks' time.
'But don't go falling off swings again,'
she said.

The End